The Alden Family Mysteries
by Gertrude Chandler Warner

THE BOXCAR CHILDREN
SURPRISE ISLAND
THE YELLOW HOUSE MYSTERY
MYSTERY RANCH
MIKE'S MYSTERY
BLUE BAY MYSTERY
THE WOODSHED MYSTERY
THE LIGHTHOUSE MYSTERY
MOUNTAIN TOP MYSTERY
SCHOOLHOUSE MYSTERY
CABOOSE MYSTERY
HOUSEBOAT MYSTERY
SNOWBOUND MYSTERY
TREE HOUSE MYSTERY
BICYCLE MYSTERY
MYSTERY IN THE SAND
MYSTERY BEHIND THE WALL
BUS STATION MYSTERY
BENNY UNCOVERS A MYSTERY

Mystery in the Sand

GERTRUDE CHANDLER WARNER

Illustrated by DAVID CUNNINGHAM

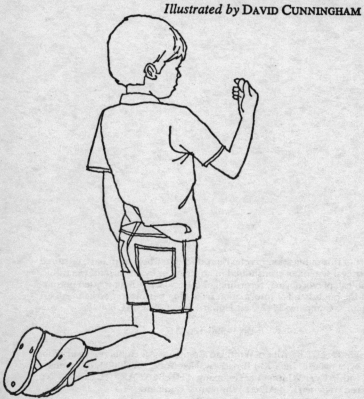

SCHOLASTIC INC.
New York Toronto London Auckland Sydney

ISBN 0-590-42673-7

Copyright © 1971 by Albert Whitman Company. All rights reserved. Published by Scholastic Inc., 730 Broadway, New York, NY 10003, by arrangements with Albert Whitman & Company. THE BOXCAR CHILDREN is a registered trademark of Albert Whitman & Company.

20 19 18 17 16 15 14 13 12 11 10   2 3 4 5/9

Printed in the U.S.A.   28

First Scholastic printing, March 1991

Contents

CHAPTER 1

Sea and Sand

Jessie Alden stood at the door. "Oh, what a beautiful morning!" she said on that hot July day.

"You can say that again, Jessie," added Benny Alden. He looked out at the blue ocean and white sand. There was not a cloud in the sky.

Violet and Henry came to the door and looked out, too. The sea gulls were sailing around a fishing boat, making a great noise.

"This is the funniest thing," said Benny. "Here we are at Aunt Jane and Uncle Andy's new trailer at the beach. A day or so ago we were at home without the least idea of going anywhere at all."

Benny called it a trailer, but it really was a mobile home. The outside was painted Aunt Jane's favorite color, blue, with white trim. Inside there was one bedroom for the two girls. Benny and his brother Henry had a double couch in the living room.

Best of all, the trailer was right on the beach. Behind it was a great space of beach grass. But in front, the Aldens could step down two steps right into the sand.

"Let's eat breakfast on the sand, Jessie," suggested Violet. "It won't be much work if we all carry our own dishes."

"I'm more than willing to carry mine," Benny said. "I'll carry them all if we can eat right away."

Henry laughed. Benny was always hungry—at home, on a trip, in the mountains, at the beach. Benny didn't change.

"Come on, Ben," Henry said. "You and I will fold up this bed into a couch."

"OK," said Benny. "Then our bedroom will look like a living room. Magic!"

In the tiny kitchen, the two girls worked fast, for they were hungry, too.

"Aunt Jane left the things we like best," said Jessie. "I'll cook the bacon and eggs, Violet, and you make the toast."

There were four trays. One was red, one was blue, one was green, and the last was violet. There was no doubt about the tray each of the Aldens would take. Jessie took the blue one, Benny took the red.

"The food is the same on every tray," Violet said. "It makes no difference what color tray."

"Oh, yes, it does, Violet," Benny objected. "I have to have red. And Henry doesn't care."

Henry laughed. He really didn't care. All he wanted was breakfast. Of course he knew that Violet should have the one that was her color.

The four Aldens sat down on the sand and began to eat their first meal at the seashore.

"I don't understand people," Violet said suddenly. She took a bite of bacon. "Everyone on this beach is sleeping. It's the best part of the day. And nobody is awake to enjoy it except us and the fishermen."

It was true. Not a person was on the beach for nearly a mile.

Benny sat cross-legged, drinking milk. He said, "I think we are the luckiest people in the world. Something is always happening to us. Right?"

"Yes," agreed Jessie. "Things seem to happen all of a sudden, so that makes it more exciting. Of course Grandfather Alden thinks up a lot of things for us to do."

"Not this time," replied Benny. "We owe this to Uncle Andy. What a man! He is so restless and always going somewhere. Then he doesn't stay very long. It's lucky Aunt Jane can keep up with him and go whenever he wants to go."

Henry said slowly, "I believe Aunt Jane thought Uncle Andy would be happy to stay here all summer. He loves to go fishing and clamming and sailing. She didn't buy this beautiful mobile home for just two weeks."

"Well, that's Uncle Andy for you," Violet said peacefully. "Just the minute he heard about that special African trip he had to get tickets and go. But it was lucky for us. We can stay here or not, just as we like."

"Just turn the key and go home when we feel

like it," Benny agreed. "It's lucky Henry has a car of his own now."

Henry laughed. "Yes, and isn't it good I picked out a car big enough for all of us?"

"That was a fine breakfast," Benny said. "It won't take long to clean up." But nobody moved.

"Look down the beach," said Henry.

Far in the distance, the Aldens saw an old man and a dog. The man was walking very slowly up the beach, with the dog at his side.

"A trained dog, I guess," said Jessie. "He stays right beside his master. I think the old man has a cane." The others thought so, too.

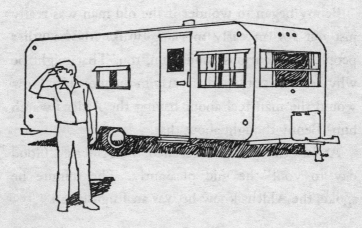

The Aldens might have picked up their trays and gone inside. But they didn't. They sat quietly, watching the old man and the dog. Once the man stopped in front of a large cottage. He seemed to rest on his cane, then to drag it along. The dog sat down near his master and waited.

"I wonder what in the world that man is doing," said Benny. "He's coming along again."

"Just taking a walk, I guess," said Jessie. "Everybody stops to pick up shells and pebbles. That's what the man is probably doing."

As the stranger came closer, the Aldens could see a ring on the end of the cane he carried. A box was fastened to the cane near the top.

Benny began to wonder if the old man was really just out for an early morning walk. Maybe other people were curious about him, too. That might be why he came out like this, early in the morning. How would the man feel about having the Aldens watch him? Benny thought about that.

At last the old man reached the Aldens. "Good day to you!" he said pleasantly. The minute he spoke, the Aldens knew he was an Englishman.

"Good morning," the four Aldens replied together.

"Is your dog friendly?" asked Benny.

"Oh, yes, don't be afraid of him. He's just big, that's all," the man answered.

Henry and Benny both got to their feet.

"Hi, feller!" said Benny, holding out a finger. The dog licked Benny's finger and then sniffed at his tray.

"Too bad," Benny said. "The bacon's all gone, boy."

Jessie looked at the stranger very carefully. She liked him at once. He had kind eyes. His wrinkles were made by smiling. He was very brown from the sun. Jessie felt as if she had always known him.

The man looked back at Jessie and said, "I came by this trailer yesterday, and I thought a man and woman lived here. Now it seems to be four young people."

Benny couldn't help thinking to himself that this man knew everything that happened on the beach.

"You are right," Jessie told him. "That was Aunt Jane and Uncle Andy Bean. This is their new mobile home. But they have gone on a trip, and we can stay here until they come back. It was a surprise to us, but that's the way we like it."

"Well, you will find this to be a beautiful beach," said the old gentleman. "My name is Daniel Lee. I walk up the beach every morning before anyone is awake. That makes a two-mile hike. It is the best part of the day."

"That's exactly what we just said," Benny exclaimed. "We said people were funny. They sleep through the best part of the day. You see, we are the only people awake on the beach, except for you and your dog."

Henry said, "I'm Henry Alden. And the one who is talking is Benny. And these are our sisters, Jessie and Violet Alden."

"Alden? Alden?" murmured their visitor. "Haven't I heard that name? It sounds familiar. A fine manufacturer of plastics?"

"That's our grandfather," Jessie said.

"Good," nodded Mr. Lee. "I hope that you will have a pleasant time in your trailer. And good day to you!"

He went off at once, with the big dog at his side.

Benny thought, "No one could do that man any harm as long as his dog is with him."

The Aldens watched Mr. Lee as he seemed to rest on his cane and then drag it over the sand.

"I never saw a cane like that, did you, Henry?" Benny asked.

"Mr. Lee doesn't really use it to help him as he walks," Violet said. "What can it be?"

"I don't know," replied Henry. "There's your mystery for our first morning, Ben."

"All right," Benny said with a laugh. "I'll find out what it is. You just wait!"

Jessie asked, "How will you do that?"

"I'll ask him," Benny replied simply. "That's the way to find out what you want to know. Go to headquarters. That's what Grandfather does."

Henry laughed. He said, "You are more like Grandfather Alden every day, Ben. I only hope Mr. Lee will answer your question, because we all want to know."

CHAPTER 2

Benny Hunts for Treasure

At last Jessie said, "Let's do the dishes and go for a swim."

Violet stood up on the sand and took her tray. She said, "You know, I can't seem to forget Mr. Lee. He seems so interesting. And he comes past here every day with his dog, he says. We'll see a lot of him. Henry, what do you think he had in his hand? I saw a dial with a pointer. It was part of the box fastened near the top of the handle."

Benny had an idea. "Is it some sort of Geiger counter?" he asked.

"No," said Henry decidedly. "Don't you remember the man at the uranium mine out at Aunt Jane's ranch? He was looking for uranium with a Geiger counter. There isn't any uranium on the beach, that's sure. This was something quite different."

Benny said, "I'll just have to ask Mr. Lee."

The Aldens all went in with their trays.

"Don't we have to go grocery shopping, Jessie?" Violet asked as she dried the spoons.

"Yes, we do," agreed Jessie. "I have looked through the refrigerator and shelves. There are one or two things we need. Milk for one thing. Ours is almost gone."

"We can't go swimming too soon after eating, anyway," Benny said. "We can do our shopping in town and then swim when we get back. It's only a quarter of a mile to town."

"It's early for an adventure in town," Henry said. But he was ready to go, too.

The Aldens put on sandals and locked the door. There stood Henry's blue car. They all climbed in, and off they went.

They did not really need the car. Beachwood was

very small, and there was just one long street. Henry drove slowly along Main Street. First came the stores, then houses began to appear on both sides. There was one big brick house with three stories and a few new houses, each with only one story.

Nothing seemed unusual until Benny said, "Oh, look at that house. It is almost a castle."

"Isn't it huge!" said Jessie. "It looks empty to me. There are no curtains in the windows at the front, even in the towers."

Henry slowed down. He said, "I wonder who built a house like that in this small town? It must have looked old-fashioned even when it was new."

Benny said, "It must have been somebody with a lot of money. Look at those towers! One, two, three, four, five towers. Nobody would buy a house like that nowadays."

"It has a sad look," Violet said. "All the new little houses look so different—like any village houses."

Henry drove very slowly down the whole of Main Street and back again. The Tower House, as all the Aldens called it, was the only house of its kind in town. There was the library, the schoolhouse, the drugstore, the fire station, and the town hall. But even the town hall was smaller than the house with the towers.

"I wonder if there are stories about that house?" Benny said as he looked back at it. "I should think the people of Beachwood would make up stories about it. I could myself. Couldn't you, Violet?"

"Yes, I could," agreed Violet, smiling. "It would be about a fairy princess held prisoner in one of the towers until she grew to be an old woman."

"We'd better keep our ears open, anyway," Benny said. "I'm sure there is something mysterious about that place."

"Let's do our shopping," Jessie suggested.

"I'm ready for a swim," Henry added.

At the supermarket, the girls bought bread, milk, bacon, hamburger, frankfurters, and a big box of dry mashed potatoes. When Henry started to pay for the groceries, he was surprised to find a small box of tea and a jar of dry coffee.

Jessie explained, "I thought we might have company sometime who might like tea or coffee. It's good to have some for times like that."

Violet, Benny, and Henry knew Jessie was thinking of the old gentleman, Mr. Lee. But they didn't say so to Jessie.

Henry drove back to the beach. The groceries were soon put away.

By the time the Aldens stepped down onto the sand, the beach was full of people. They could see different colors of swimsuits far up and down the beach. Some people were in the water and some were lying on the beach to get a tan. Children were screaming just for the fun of it.

The Aldens joined the swimmers and spent the rest of the morning in the cool salt water.

That evening, Benny thought about walking over toward Beachwood. Would there be any lights in the old house with the five towers? Maybe he was trying too hard to find a mystery.

The next morning, early, Benny found someone had set up a chair on the beach. He smiled when he found a tray all set with a teacup, a few strips of bread and butter on a small plate, and a fat black teapot. Already, it seemed, Mr. Lee was part of the beach family.

The Aldens waited. They were not disappointed. As they finished breakfast on the sand, they saw Mr. Lee and his dog coming up the beach. Jessie ran into the kitchen to set the water boiling on the stove. She waited, however, to see whether Mr. Lee wanted tea or coffee.

As the old gentleman reached the Aldens, he saw the chair and smiled. "I wonder if this is for me?" he asked, sitting down and looking at the family.

"Yes, it is," said Benny. "I suppose you have had breakfast?"

"Yes, I eat very early," Mr. Lee replied. "I don't sleep too well."

Jessie called from the door, "Could you drink another cup of tea or coffee?"

"Yes, indeed. Tea, please. An Englishman can always drink a cup of hot tea."

Jessie noticed the word "hot" so she made sure that the little teapot was hot before she poured in the boiling water. She carried the tray to the beach.

She said, "I read somewhere that the English like milk instead of cream in their tea."

"That is correct, young lady," said Mr. Lee. He

drank the hot tea and ate all the bread and butter.

Benny watched him as he poured a second cup of tea. Benny wanted to ask Mr. Lee about the cane he carried. And Mr. Lee might know something about the Tower House, too. It was hard to know what to ask about first, and Benny wanted to be polite, too.

He said, "I can't understand why anyone likes tea. It tastes so awful. And will you tell us—is your cane some kind of Geiger counter?"

Mr. Lee didn't seem surprised at the question. "No," he replied. "It is a metal-finder, which is quite different. Some people call it a treasure-finder, and that may be true. And now I will tell you a secret, although no one else knows it. But first I must tell you that hundreds of people come here in the summer. Some are rich and some are not, and I'm sorry to say a good many are not very careful."

"About water safety?" asked Violet.

Mr. Lee smiled. "No, they are careful about that. But someone has a watch or piece of jewelry. Before swimming, he takes it off and leaves it on the beach."

"I begin to see," said Jessie, nodding.

"I'm sure you do. But just the same, it is surprising

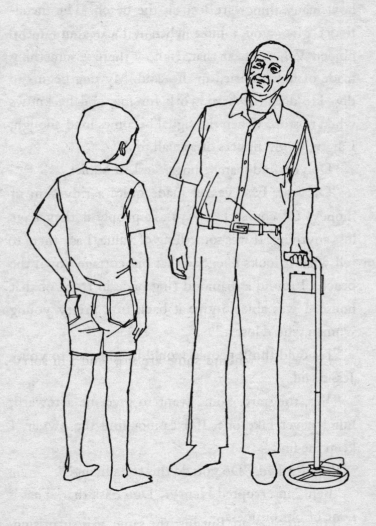

how many things are lost on the beach. The metal-finder gives you a buzz when it locates any metal object. When I hear that, I know there is something made of metal buried in the sand. My dog begins to dig. He does the hard work for me, and he knows when to stop. When the signal becomes loud enough, I dig with my fingers or a small tool."

"Do you find many things?" asked Violet.

"Oh, yes. Last year I made quite a tidy sum of money. Of course I always ask people if they have lost anything. If it is something of value, I ask them to tell what it looks like. See that big cottage down the beach? I found a diamond ring once in front of that house. I was able to give it back to a pretty young woman who'd lost it."

"I should think people would be grateful to you," Jessie said.

"Yes, they are. Some want to give me a reward, but I never take one. If I cannot find the owner, I keep the find."

Benny asked, "Do you do this for a living?"

"Ben!" interrupted Henry. "Don't ask that. That is none of our business."

Mr. Lee laughed. "I don't mind telling Benny. I think I could make a living this way, but I don't. This just gives me something to do. I am too old to go on with my regular work."

No one asked Mr. Lee what his regular work had been. He drank the last of the tea and said, "I brought down a bracelet to show you. I found it just last week. I have cleaned off the sand." He took it out of his pocket and handed it to Jessie.

She said, "I don't know much about jewelry, but this looks like a good bracelet to me."

"It's beautiful," Violet said.

"It is," Mr. Lee agreed. "I should say it is worth quite a bit. So far I can't find the owner. You see, people come to this beach from faraway places. They stay for a few days or a week, or sometimes just for a day. It is very hard to trace them."

Benny suddenly remembered something he had heard Uncle Andy say. He winked at Mr. Lee and said, "You do your best. And that's all an old horse can do. Uncle Andy says his grandfather said that."

Mr. Lee laughed. "Thank you, Benny," he said. "Now would you like to try the metal-finder?"

"Would I?" exclaimed Benny. "I might find a watch."

"So you might," agreed Mr. Lee. "And you might find nothing. Just drag the circle on the end of the rod over the sand. Slowly, slowly!"

Benny took the handle. Here was an adventure coming right to him.

Mr. Lee stepped out of the way.

"Don't get too excited, Ben," said Henry.

"I'm not excited at all," said Benny. "See how cool I am?"

There was a small green box on the handle of the rod. It had a clock face with a needle that trembled. It also made a buzzing sound.

The big dog stood up. He didn't understand why a strange boy was using his master's rod.

"It's all right, Richard," Mr. Lee said to the dog. "Lie down again. This boy will do your digging."

"Richard?" repeated Henry, laughing. "The dog's name is Richard?"

"Yes, I named him for the man who bought the biggest diamond in the world. Sometimes I find diamond jewelry in the sand."

Benny slowly dragged the metal-finder over the sand. They all watched him, and even Henry was excited. All at once the finder began to make a sound, louder and louder.

"You've found something, Benny," Mr. Lee said calmly. "Do you want to dig with your hands?"

"Yes!" Benny answered. "I haven't a shovel."

Benny knelt down and began to dig the dry sand away from the spot. Violet went quietly into the trailer and came back with a large old spoon. Benny took it gladly. He could dig faster. The sound grew louder and louder.

"Don't expect too much, Benny," warned Mr. Lee. "You may only find an old tin can. The treasure-finder can't tell the difference between junk and something valuable."

Benny threw out spoonfuls of wet sand now, and the hole was quite a deep one.

Mr. Lee said, "If you find something solid, rub it between your fingers. Don't get excited. It may be just a stone with iron ore in it."

Benny sat back. He had something between his fingers.

"Well, here is something anyway," he said. "It may be a stone, but I don't think it is. It could be a quarter or maybe a gold piece. It's round and flat."

Benny rubbed off the sand. The thing in his hand was shiny, but it was no coin—not even a penny.

"Oh, no!" Benny said. "It's just an old bottle cap."

Jessie drew a long breath. "Mr. Lee warned us, Benny," she said. "But it was fun to think it might be something important. Don't be discouraged."

"Right," said Mr. Lee. "You have the idea now. Maybe it was a good thing not to find anything. If you had, you would always think it was easy. It takes a lot of patience. Some day you can try again."

"Yes, I know," said Benny. "Then I'll find a twin bottle cap for this one."

They all laughed.

"I'll see you tomorrow," said Mr. Lee, getting up. "Thank you again for the tea."

The Aldens watched him as he walked up the beach with Richard.

Benny said, "He seems like one of the family, doesn't he?"

"And we've known him for only two days," Jessie said.

"Interesting things happen to us, no matter where we go!" Benny exclaimed. "We must be magnetic."

"And attract adventures," Henry said with a laugh.

Benny looked down at the spoon he still held in his hand. It was covered with sand. "I'll run down to the water and wash this off," he said. "I'd rather wash dishes this way than in a kitchen."

The other Aldens picked up the trays and went into their trailer house. Benny looked up and down the beach. Mr. Lee and Richard were already in the distance. No one else was to be seen in either direction.

"And yet," Benny said to himself, "here are fresh-looking footprints right at the water's edge. The tide washed the whole beach clean in the night. Now where did these footprints come from?"

Benny shook his head. Someone else must be up and out on the beach even earlier than Mr. Lee. Benny tried to guess whether the footprints had been made by a man or a woman. When he looked closely, he saw two sets of footprints.

"Funny," Benny decided. "One set of footprints looks small, almost as if they belong to a boy. Now I wonder."

Benny washed off the spoon. As he stood up, he decided not to tell Henry or the girls about the footprints, at least not yet. After all, they might be like his treasure hunting. They might not mean a thing, just the way his find was nothing but a bottle cap.

However, Benny planned to keep his eyes open for any early morning visitors to the beach.

CHAPTER 3

Midnight Mystery

At midnight, Benny woke up suddenly. He felt strange. "What's the matter with me?" he thought.

Then Benny saw the moon was shining right in his face. It was almost as bright as day. Without waking Henry, Benny slipped out of bed to pull the curtain across the window.

For a minute Benny stood looking out at the beach and the dark water with the bright streak of moonlight on it. Then he stepped quickly back from the window, for somebody was on the beach.

As Benny carefully peered out, he saw two dark figures looking at the trailer house. They were too far away and near the water for Benny to see them very well.

"Now what is going on?" Benny asked himself. "Two people looking at our house." He tried to tell whether the figures were men or women. "I guess they are men," he thought. "They have on pants."

One of the walkers on the beach was much smaller than the other. Could it be a man and a boy? But at that moment Benny remembered that everybody at the beach dressed in pants—men, women, boys, and girls.

The two men (if they were men) still stood looking at the trailer. Then one bent over and pointed at the sand, and the two seemed to talk.

Benny wished he could hear what they said. The beach was very quiet, but the water made enough noise to cover the sound of the voices.

"Can they be looking for something?" Benny wondered. "Anyway they are up to no good. I wonder if I ought to wake Henry? I think so."

Henry was awake at once. "What's the matter, Ben?" he whispered.

"I don't know. See those two men looking at our trailer? What are they doing on the beach at midnight?"

"Well, they certainly are not just taking a walk," whispered Henry. "We'll watch and see what they do next."

The boys tried to see the two figures more plainly, but their clothes were dark, and they were fifty feet or more away.

"Look at that, Henry!" Benny said softly. "Quick! Get out of sight."

The two men were pointing at a spot in the sand. One looked toward the trailer, then got down and began to dig. But the digging did not last long.

At last the two figures seemed to give up. They turned and walked up the beach, looking back as they walked. That was all the boys could see.

"Look, Ben!" whispered Henry suddenly. "Another man!"

As the first two walkers hurried more quickly up the beach, another figure followed at a distance. It seemed to be a man who wore a long cape. He was certainly following the first two. All at once he began to run.

"He is trying to catch the other two!" Benny whispered in excitement.

"Trying to catch up, anyway," agreed Henry. The man's cape flapped in the wind. "This is very strange, the whole thing. I don't think we need to be afraid, Ben. There are lots of neighbors near us."

The boys still watched the three figures. A dog howled in the distance.

Then the first two men turned off the sand into the beach grass and walked away out of sight. The man in the cape stood still and watched for a minute. Then he turned around and started back.

"Wait!" said Henry in a low voice. "He will go right past us on his way back. Maybe we can see more then."

Soon the figure went by at a fast pace, but the two boys could not see anything more. He was too far away, down by the water.

"I wish I could see better," Henry said.

Benny whispered, "That long cape covers him up. It could be a woman and not a man at all."

"Maybe they are all women," returned Henry. That seemed so funny that the boys laughed softly. They watched until the last figure had gone down the beach. His steps were slow now.

"I hope whoever it is won't bother Mr. Lee," said Benny, feeling worried.

"Mr. Lee can take care of himself," said Henry. "Don't forget he has the dog."

"That's right. I forgot Richard. If anyone tried to hurt his master, Richard would tear him to pieces. I guess that's the end of this adventure."

Benny remembered the footprints he had seen in the sand in the morning, but all at once he was too sleepy to think about anything.

The two boys went back to bed. They slept until morning, when they heard Jessie in the kitchen getting breakfast. They told her about their excitement at midnight.

After breakfast on the sand, with tea ready, the Aldens were not surprised to see Mr. Lee coming toward them. But he walked slowly. When he arrived, he said "Good day" as usual, but he looked tired.

Jessie thought, "Oh, I do hope he isn't sick. He looks terrible this morning."

"You had a bad night?" she asked as she put the teapot on the tray.

"Yes, I really did. I am not a good sleeper, anyway. Are you?" He looked right at Jessie as he said this. It was almost like asking her if she had seen the men walking around on the beach.

"We are all good sleepers," replied Jessie. "I'm so sorry you have such bad nights. Nothing bothers me, unless I hear somebody calling 'Jessie.' Then I wake right up."

Mr. Lee drank his tea as if he needed it. And after a short time he began to look better. He smiled at the Aldens, perhaps because he could see that they were worried about him.

Suddenly Mr. Lee asked, "Benny, why don't you try the metal-finder again? Perhaps you'll find something, perhaps you won't. It's always the same chance when you try."

"I understand," Benny replied. He took up the metal-finder and looked around at the beach.

Mr. Lee said, "Do you see that piece of post? I'm quite sure there used to be an old dock there because there are several posts like that. Try listening around them. You see, objects usually work their way under the sand to a post or a big rock. Go slowly now."

Benny obeyed. He ran the ring very, very slowly around the post. Richard stood up. He wagged his tail, but he didn't understand why this strange boy should be using his master's rod again. He lay down and whined.

All at once the metal-finder gave a signal that something was nearby.

"Yes," nodded Mr. Lee, "you've found something. Start digging."

Benny was only too willing to dig. Richard started to get up and then lay down again. Benny went on digging as fast as he could. "You want to dig, Henry?" he asked.

"No, I'd rather watch you," said Henry.

When the hole was fairly deep, one of Benny's fingers touched something. He reached in and picked up a round object, covered with wet sand. "Probably another bottle top," he said, "or the cover of a little jar." He gave it to Mr. Lee.

With one rub of his fingers, Mr. Lee pushed away the sand and said, "It looks like an old watch. Take it yourself, Benny. You found it, whatever it is."

Violet handed Benny one of her paint brushes and

he carefully brushed off the sand. "It's a gold locket!" he exclaimed. "How about *that?*"

"Well, well," Mr. Lee said, much pleased. "You have had good luck on your second try. Now is the time to be careful."

"Shall we go into the house?" asked Jessie.

"Yes, I think that would be wise," replied Mr. Lee. "Then if anything drops off the locket, we won't lose it in the sand."

The Aldens and Mr. Lee and Richard, the dog, all went into the small living room of the trailer. Henry took the books off a little table and moved it in front of Mr. Lee.

"You'd better show us what to do this time," Henry said. "We don't know anything about this."

Mr. Lee took a small box from his pocket and opened it. It held a strange set of tools. He spread out a piece of thin black silk. He put the locket on top, and a magnifying glass in his eye.

"You look like a watchmaker," Benny said.

Mr. Lee looked closely at the locket and then exclaimed, "Look, there are initials on the cover: R.L."

"R.L.," repeated Jessie. "That should make it easier to find the owner."

"Don't be too sure," Mr. Lee said. "It may take a long time."

Then with great care, he began to brush both sides of the locket. "I won't open it just yet," he explained. "I want to get all the sand out of the edges first."

"Is it a good locket?" asked Benny.

Mr. Lee was using a fine tool to pick out bits of sand along the crack where the locket opened. He said, "Yes, I think it is quite good. It is probably gold for one thing, and it is old. And for another thing, we may find a puzzle when we open it."

"Oh, we love mysteries," Benny exclaimed. "I do hope there's a mystery inside."

With a very fine tool Mr. Lee gently pried up the cover of the locket, first on one side and then on the other. At last the locket came open, but not enough to show what, if anything, was inside.

Mr. Lee looked up at Benny. "From now on, it is yours, Benny. You found it. You take it. See what's inside."

"You take it, Violet," said Benny. "Your fingers are better with little things than mine are."

Violet did not hold back. She sat down on the couch as Mr. Lee moved over. Very gently she opened the locket.

"Pictures!" she said. "One of a house, and one of a cat."

Jessie looked over Violet's shoulder. "Those pictures look old and faded," she said. "But the *house* —look, Benny!"

Benny cried, "The house is the one with the towers!"

"I believe you are right," Jessie said. "The picture shows only one tower, but I'm sure that is the house here in Beachwood."

Mr. Lee took one look. He said, "One tower or not, that's the Tower House on Main Street."

Benny looked a little unhappy. "How easy to solve this mystery," he said. "A picture of a cat and a picture of the Tower House and R.L. on the cover. The answers are all right here in Beachwood. Just a quarter of a mile away, and there's the owner."

But later on, Benny decided the mystery was more

than a quarter of a mile away. And if Benny had looked quickly at Mr. Lee, he might have seen a little smile come and go. Perhaps Mr. Lee guessed the mystery would not be so easy to solve.

After Mr. Lee had put away his tools, he called his dog, picked up his treasure-finder and said good-bye.

CHAPTER 4

Are Finders Keepers?

Benny held the locket, turning it over in his hand. "I think we ought to go right to Beachwood and return the locket," he said.

"Not so fast, Ben," said Henry. "Maybe the locket doesn't belong to the people who live there now. If there *are* any people—you remember how empty the Tower House looked."

"Well, we can ask somebody who lives there," Benny agreed. "Maybe the man in the drugstore knows who lives there. Drugstore men know everything, and besides, the Tower House is almost across the street."

Jessie said, "Let's go. There isn't much to do here except lie around in the sand, and I don't think much of that."

"And I am curious about that picture of a cat," Violet said. "Why not the picture of a person?"

Violet put away the few dishes, and Jessie swept out the tiny kitchen. Henry locked the trailer home and they drove to Beachwood.

Henry parked the car at the drugstore and they all went in. They were lucky about two things. There was nobody else in the store, and the clerk behind the counter was a great talker.

First, the Aldens bought some writing paper and some suntan oil. Then Benny said, "May I ask you a question?"

"Sure thing. Fire away," replied the clerk. "You are staying in the new Andy Bean trailer down on the shore, aren't you?"

"Well, yes, we are," Benny answered. He was surprised to find the clerk knew so much about the Aldens. He did not think the clerk could have seen them before. On their first shopping trip to Beachwood, the Aldens had only gone to the supermarket.

But news travels fast in a small town.

"We want to ask you about that Tower House across the street," Benny said.

"Oho," said the clerk. "That is easy in one way. I know as much as anybody—but nobody knows very much. It's a queer sort of place."

"I see," said Benny. "Who lives there? Who owns it?"

"I don't know who owns it. As to who lives there, I'll tell you all I know. Most of the house is empty. But on the first floor of one of the back towers there is a woman living alone. She is about fifty years old. She says her name is Mary Smith, but I don't believe a word of it myself. There is something funny about her."

The Aldens looked at each other. This was beginning to sound more and more interesting.

"This Mary Smith never comes out except to buy things to eat and to go to the post office. That's always on a Wednesday. She looks well, but she never smiles. And she won't say a word unless she has to. She just picks up her vegetables and meat in the supermarket and pays for them. One thing makes you wonder about her. She buys a lot of cheap meat. I don't see how she can eat it. Once in a while she comes in here for aspirin. That's about it."

"This is Wednesday," said Jessie. "Maybe we can talk to her today."

"She won't talk," said the man, shaking his head. "She'll cut you off in some way. And you would have to wait a long time. She comes late in the afternoon, after the crowd has gone."

"Maybe it would be better to knock on her door," said Violet. "What would happen then?"

"She wouldn't come to the door. You can be sure of that. At least she never has. A few people tried it long ago. They wanted to be friendly, but she never came to the door. So nobody goes now."

"There's always a first time," Benny said. "I'd rather talk to her at her own house than in a store anyway."

"Well, if you have something you really want to talk to her about," said the clerk, "I suppose you can try. No harm done, unless you get your feelings hurt. I'd like to see you try, I really would."

Benny was thinking to himself that the clerk must

wonder why the Aldens wanted to see Mary Smith. But he was not going to say anything to explain.

"I think we will try to see her," said Jessie. "We really want to. Thank you for your help."

As the Aldens went down the street, Benny said, "He did help us, and he never asked us why we wanted to talk to Miss Smith."

"But he was dying to know," Henry agreed. "And I don't blame him. Let's walk over and knock at that door at the side of the Tower House."

As the Aldens came nearer, they could see that the house did indeed look empty except for the first floor of one of the back towers. There were curtains in the windows and at the door. They looked thick and were a dark color.

"I'm just as glad we are coming in the daylight," Violet said. "There is something spooky about this old house."

Henry said, "Do you have the locket, Benny?"

"It's in my pocket, wrapped in a paper," Benny said. "I don't want to show it until Miss Smith describes it."

Jessie looked at the house and said almost in a whisper, "I have a feeling we are being watched. Don't you feel that way, too?"

"There are four of us and just one Miss Smith," Benny said. "There's nothing to worry about." But just the same Benny said, "Henry, you rap at the door."

Henry knocked. Nothing happened.

"Just what the man said would happen," Benny said. "Try again, Henry."

Henry tried a fancy rap: *Da*-da-da-*Dum*-da.

The Aldens waited. Then to their surprise the door slowly opened and a woman looked at the visitors.

What a cold, grim face, without a sign of a smile!

Benny thought, "She'd be nice looking if she was even the least bit friendly." Her face was round and very fair. Her hair was light brown and curly, but pulled straight back into a tight knot. She did not even ask, "What do you want?"

Henry spoke for all the Aldens. "You are Miss Smith?" he asked. "Miss Mary Smith?"

The woman nodded.

"We found something down on the beach," Henry went on. "It was buried in the sand. We think it has something to do with this house."

Benny's hand closed around the locket in the paper, but he left it in his pocket.

The woman looked quickly and sharply from one of the visitors to the next. Then she said, "I haven't lost anything. Please don't bother me."

She shut the door, and the Aldens heard the key turn in the lock.

"Well, that is too bad," said Violet, really feeling

hurt. "I'm sorry for anyone like that. She must be very unhappy."

Benny was thinking fast. As they walked away from the Tower House he said, "Two things. First, the initials on the locket are R.L. That doesn't fit with Mary Smith. And second, did you notice that smell when the door was opened? What was it?"

Henry wrinkled his nose. "You are right, Benny," he said. "There was a strong smell—for a minute I thought of a zoo, or a circus. What could it be?"

"Maybe we'll never know," said Violet.

"Oh, yes, we will, Violet," Benny said quickly. "You just wait. Have we ever given up on a mystery? And this one is the easiest of all. You'll see."

Henry looked at Benny and laughed. "All right, what do you plan to do next, Benny?"

"How about lunch?" Benny asked. "I saw two or three places on Main Street where they serve meals. I want a piece of apple pie. My head works better when my stomach is full."

Jessie looked back at the Tower House. Nothing was changed. No one was watching from a dark window. But Jessie felt uneasy just the same.

CHAPTER 5

A Hundred Cats!

The Aldens found a small restaurant on Main Street. There was a large sign with an apple painted on it.

"The Red Apple," Benny said. "This place ought to have apple pie, don't you think?"

The Aldens went in, and the girl showed them to a table for four.

Jessie said, "Let's have something I can't cook in the trailer kitchen."

"Roast lamb and baked potato for me," Henry said. "You could never roast lamb in our oven. And I am hungry after all the excitement of last night and this day."

They all agreed on lamb—all but Benny. "No," he said, "I'll stick to my hamburgers and peanut butter sandwiches."

"Benny," objected Jessie, "why have the same old thing? You can have a change."

"I don't like a change," answered Benny. "I like peanut butter, and for dessert, apple pie and cheese."

"Well, sandwiches *are* cheaper," said Henry.

The food was delicious, and the waitress pleasant. She laughed at Benny with his peanut butter. She said, "I've got a young brother like you. He never gets tired of peanut butter and jelly."

"Oh, I forgot the jelly," Benny replied. "I'd like that, too."

As the Aldens were eating, the manager came up to their table and asked if everything was all right.

"Oh, yes," replied Jessie. She noticed that the manager was an older man and that gave her an idea. "We are curious about that Tower House," she said. "It is so different from anything else in town. Do you know who lives there and who owns it?"

"Well," answered the manager, "I don't remember the Lane family myself, but I think the house is still owned by the Lanes. But then I may be wrong. I think all the Lanes are dead. Miss Mary Smith lives there all alone."

At the mention of the name *Lane*, Benny looked up quickly. Could the L on the locket stand for Lane? That surely seemed a good guess.

"Do you remember when Miss Smith moved in?" asked Henry.

"Well, yes and no, you might say," the manager answered.

"I guess you mean you were too young to remember," said Benny.

The man laughed. "No, I am not too young. I was right here when suddenly, just like that, Miss Mary Smith lived in the Tower House. She came in the night and nobody saw her move in. When morning came, bang! there she was."

"You see her around Beachwood?" Jessie asked.

"She comes out once in a while to buy food or to go to the post office. That's about all. I'd say she just doesn't like people."

"That's funny," said Benny. "I can't understand that."

The manager smiled at Benny and said, "Well, you like everybody. That's why you can't understand."

But Benny did not quite agree. He said, "I think everyone likes people. But some people don't know that they do."

"Maybe you are right," the older man said. "I have an aunt who never smiles, but it is because she is shy."

"We have a special reason for wanting to talk to Miss Smith," Henry told the manager. And he explained about the locket with the picture of the Tower House in it.

"And the L must stand for Lane," Benny added. "You have already helped us."

"I'm surprised Miss Smith even opened the door," the man said. "She is a strange person. Now, understand—I don't know this for a fact—but I think Miss Smith is an artist and paints pictures."

Benny looked surprised. "Why?" he asked. "Why do you think so?"

"About every month or so, I know that Miss Smith mails a package to New York. I understand it always goes to the same address, which is on one of the avenues where dealers buy and sell paintings. Pictures come through in a special kind of box. I used to work in a city post office, and that's how I know. Miss Smith uses the same kind of box."

"Miss Smith may be a painter," Violet said thoughtfully.

"I don't know what she paints," the man said. "She hardly ever goes out. She doesn't look around her or paint the sea or houses."

Violet said, "A real artist can paint anything and sell it. A door or a window or an old chair."

Benny said, "Even a design in a carpet."

The man laughed. "I suppose you're right. Anyway if she is an artist, that is probably the way she earns money."

"Wouldn't you think she would want people to see her work?" asked Violet. "She sounds so odd."

The manager went on slowly and his voice was low. "I do hear all sorts of wild stories about Miss Smith. Of course I am not ready to believe them. But I have heard that she keeps a hundred cats in that tower."

"A hundred cats!" exclaimed Jessie. "I can't believe that many, but maybe one or two."

"Or no cats at all," added the manager. "People like to make up stories about anyone they don't understand."

Benny said, "I bet she does keep cats. When she opened the door, we were standing near enough to smell something. It really smelled like the lion house at the zoo. What a smell!"

The manager looked at Benny. "That is the first real proof I have ever heard that there might really be cats at the Tower House. People are often a lot like their pets. Miss Smith is like a cat, very quiet."

"What makes you say that?" asked Benny.

"When she buys stamps and envelopes, she has a little paper she gives to the clerk, saying how many stamps she wants and what kind. Miss Smith doesn't have to say a word. She pays for them and goes out. She always seems to have money."

"But I should think she would be interested in a locket that has a picture of her own house," Benny said. He felt there was a puzzle here he should be able to solve. "Would you like to see the locket?"

"Indeed I would," said the man. He held the locket and then opened it carefully.

"Well," he said in surprise. "You didn't tell me there was a picture of a cat inside. I am sure that this cat must have died long ago. But probably Miss Smith has a young cat a lot like this. Who knows?" He laughed.

Benny put the locket back in his pocket.

Henry said, "I guess we'll have to think what to do next. You have helped us a lot. Now we have some idea of what Miss Smith does to keep busy."

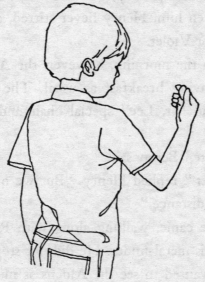

Jessie said, "Let's go back to the beach. We've done enough today."

On the way back to the trailer, Benny said, "I can't wait to tell Mr. Lee what we have learned so far."

"I wonder if we'll see anyone walking on the beach at midnight," said Henry.

Violet said, "I hope not!"

Benny really meant to wake up during the night. He wanted to see if anyone would be on the beach at midnight. But he swam so much that he slept very soundly. Nothing as quiet as footsteps in the sand could waken him. Henry never stirred, and neither did Jessie or Violet.

Early in the morning, however, the Aldens were outside, having breakfast as usual. The kettle was boiling, and Mr. Lee's special chair and cup were ready.

"He's late," Benny said.

"Not yet," replied Henry. "But we ought to see him in the distance."

Then he came, walking along with Richard and carrying his metal-finder. He did not stop often because he wanted to see the Aldens as much as they wanted to see him. He walked faster and was soon near enough to speak.

"How did you get along in town?" he called.

"Quite well," said Jessie, pouring the hot tea.

"You are spoiling me," said the old gentleman. "When you go home, I shall miss my extra breakfast. Do tell me what you did."

One by one, the Aldens told about Miss Smith's closing the door in their faces, about the Red Apple, the manager's ideas, and the cats.

Mr. Lee nodded. "The manager is right about the cat in the picture. It can't be living now. But it was surely a beautiful cat."

"We're going to see if we can find out more about Miss Smith," Benny said. "I still wonder why she didn't even want to see the locket."

"Mr. Lee, what did you do while we were gone?" asked Jessie.

"Oh, I was going to tell you," he said, fishing in his pocket. He took out a very large coin. "I found this buried two feet down, right in front of the biggest cottage. It is a very old coin and I should think valuable."

The Aldens looked at the old coin. "Think how long this has been lost!" exclaimed Jessie.

"Yes," said Mr. Lee. "It may have been lost way up under the cottage long before there was a house there. It probably worked its way downhill. I have marked the place. I shall dig deeper there this winter and may find other things. There is no one around to bother me when the weather is cold."

"Someone at the cottage didn't lose that coin?" asked Violet.

"No, I'm sure not. They have been here only a week, and the coin was buried deep. It was lost a long time ago. Once I found a 1937 buffalo nickel. That is a very special coin, too. And yesterday I found a Boy Scout pin. It belonged to the boy in the house next to mine. That was the best part of my day—to see his face when I gave him his pin."

The Aldens couldn't help but notice that the best part of Mr. Lee's adventure had been finding the Boy Scout pin, not the valuable coin.

CHAPTER 6

Benny to the Rescue

After Mr. Lee had gone, Benny said, "I'll tell you what let's do. Let's drive around *behind* the Tower House. If we go very slowly maybe we can see a back window. We wouldn't seem to be looking."

"Fine," said Henry. "I can't believe those stories about a hundred cats are true."

"Maybe they are, Henry," said Jessie. "Remember that strong smell."

"Let's go," said Benny. He took his tray into the kitchen, and the others followed.

Soon the Aldens were driving up a beach road they had not taken before. It suddenly turned to the right.

"I guess nobody uses this road," said Henry. "We've met no cars or people."

"Slower!" said Benny. "Just crawl along, and then we can see."

But there was not much to see, even though Henry drove as slowly as he could. Large trees stood at the back and sides of the Tower House. Everything looked wild and as if no one cared.

All at once the Aldens saw two small boys. They had towels around their shoulders. They were going to the beach. The boys noticed the Aldens looking toward the Tower House.

"Hey!" called one of the boys. "Going to see the old witch?"

Henry stopped the car. "Old witch?" he asked.

"Yeah," replied the boy, pointing to the Tower House. The upper floors of all the towers were boarded up. "Don't you know an old witch lives there with one hundred cats?"

Violet said in a quiet voice, "How do you know?"

"Everybody knows. Ask anybody."

The other boy said, "I know I'd never go there. Not on a bet."

Jessie said, "We saw the woman who lives there. Her name is Miss Mary Smith."

"Aw, you saw her by daylight, going grocery shopping. You never saw her running on the beach at night, I bet. She goes to howl at the moon."

"Nonsense!" said Jessie. "Nobody howls at the moon, except maybe dogs."

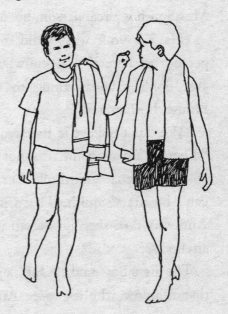

"You're sure of yourself, aren't you? Well, we're warning you. Don't hang around this house. She can put a hex on you as easy as looking at you. And she's got those hundred cats. Cats can be crazy, too. She feeds them raw meat."

"Doesn't she buy cat food?" asked Violet.

"Naw, never. She buys raw meat, pounds of it, and that makes them wild. Didn't you ever hear of an old witch and her cats?"

"Yes, on Halloween," answered Henry. "But Miss Smith is a real person, not a witch."

"Have it your way," said the other boy. "You'll get out of here if you know what's good for you. Just don't have anything to do with the Tower House. It's haunted."

"We don't believe in haunted houses," said Benny. "There is always some reason if you can just find it."

"That's what you think. For one thing, her name can't be Mary Smith. That's just a made-up name. And why does she shut herself up and never speak to anybody?"

The first boy said, "One day I threw a stone at that window, the big one. And you know what?

Mary Smith got a big piece of glass and lugged it home and put it in herself. Never said a word about it to anybody."

"You think that was crazy?" asked Benny.

"Yes, I do. Anybody else would have told the police. But she didn't. You know why? She doesn't want the police to know too much about *her*. She'd rather pay for that big window pane and fix it herself."

Henry asked, "Why did you break her window, anyway?"

"Well, I just felt like throwing a stone, and the kid with me said to go ahead. He'd like to see what she would do about it."

"And you found out," Benny nodded. "I'm sorry for Miss Smith or whoever she is. That glass must have cost plenty. It must have been heavy, too."

"The old witch has money, that's for sure," said the boy. "She buys lots of food for herself. I'm not sorry for her. You can be sorry if you like, not me."

And the two boys went off, swinging their towels.

The Aldens sat perfectly still in the car. At last Jessie spoke slowly. "Of course Miss Smith isn't a witch. But there is something very wrong about her. I wish I knew what it was."

"Yes," agreed Benny. "I don't know why she didn't take the locket. She could have looked at it anyway. But she just shut her door."

The Aldens looked toward the big window behind the bushes. There was no curtain. Nothing moved inside. There was no sound.

"Everything looks so hot and dry," Jessie said. "Even the weeds look brown."

"I suppose we're just wasting our time," Violet said at last. "Let's go and do our grocery shopping, Henry."

Henry began to back the car to turn it around on the narrow back road. Suddenly Benny heard something.

"Hey, Henry, did you hear that? Me-ow! That was a cat. Stop again."

"I didn't hear anything," replied Henry. "The car makes such a racket backing on these stones."

"Well, I did," said Benny. "I heard meow just as plain as anything."

The family waited. Nobody else heard anything.

And even Benny heard nothing more. They turned around and watched the window again.

"Was that a shadow?" whispered Jessie.

"It looked like a shadow," whispered Benny.

Then a pure white cat jumped up on the windowsill behind the glass. "Mee-ow," it cried.

"There!" exclaimed Benny. "There is one of the hundred cats for you!"

"What a beauty," whispered Violet. "Pure white. I wish I could see his eyes. He looks so soft and furry. And look at his big tail."

The cat sat down on the windowsill and began to wash its paws. The Aldens could see him plainly.

Violet said, "I think that is a Persian cat."

Benny said, "Now we know there is at least one cat in the Tower House. Maybe there are ninety-nine more hidden away."

Henry said, "We've been here quite a long time. If anyone besides the cat in the Tower House has seen us, it might not be good. After all, we don't want Miss Smith to think we are spying on her."

"I didn't think of that," said Jessie. "Yes, let's go."

Jessie and Violet did the shopping. The boys

walked along Main Street, looking in the windows. There were all sorts of things for the summer people to buy. An art store had oil paintings of the ocean. Then the boys crossed the street.

Most of the buildings on that side were made of wood, and some were quite close together.

Henry and Benny came to the fire station. Benny waved at one of the firemen. "Hot, isn't it?" he called.

The fireman nodded. "Bad weather for firemen," he said. "Everything is so dry. This is when a fire can spread fast."

"Come on, Benny," Henry said. "Let's go back to the car. The girls should have their shopping done now."

Jessie and Violet were waiting. "I'm going for a swim as soon as we get back," Violet said, getting into the car.

"Let's just take one more look at the Tower House on our way back," Benny said.

As the car came near the old house, Henry slowed down. All at once Benny exclaimed, "Stop, Henry! Stop right here."

Before anyone could say a word Benny had the car door open and had jumped out. He was running back along Main Street as fast as he could.

"What—" Henry started to say. Then he stopped. At that moment Violet said, "Henry, I smell something burning!"

"Me, too," Jessie said.

Henry and the girls jumped out of the car and looked around. The car was safe. But why had Benny run off? Now he had disappeared.

Suddenly Violet said, "Look, Henry! The grass in the yard is on fire!"

As she spoke, a flame reached the bushes. The dry leaves blazed up high.

"Get back!" Henry said. "I'll go for help."

But help was already there. The fire engine pulled in just as Henry started. Benny came racing after it.

Jessie exclaimed, "Oh, that's where Benny was. He smelled smoke and ran back for the firemen."

Even before Benny reached the girls, a fireman was turning a chemical fire extinguisher on the bushes. Another fireman was beating out the grass fire.

Everyone was so busy that they did not see the side door of the Tower House open just a crack. No one saw that there were now three cats on the windowsill of the big back window.

Nobody thought that Miss Smith, inside the house, could hear every word.

The fire blazed high for a moment, and then it began to die down. Before anyone walking past could call, "Fire! Fire!" the danger was over.

The fire chief came over to the Aldens. He said, "This was only a small brush fire. Only the bushes and the grass burned. But in fifteen minutes it would have been a big house fire. This house could have burned to the ground. Then the fire could have spread to the next row of houses on the hill. The wind is blowing the right way for that. You saved Miss Smith's house, and maybe her life, young man." He looked at Benny.

Benny said slowly, "People don't seem to like Miss Smith. Do you think somebody started the fire?"

"No, I don't think so," the fireman answered. "Maybe someone threw a cigaret in the bushes."

"Here you are," said another fireman. "Here's the end of a cigaret right at the edge of the grass."

"People are so careless," the first fireman said. "If this had happened at night, the whole town of Beachwood could have burned."

There was still a smoky smell in the air, but the fire was out. The firemen went back to their truck.

"Good work," the fire chief said to Benny. "You ran for help. You didn't waste any time trying to put the fire out by yourself."

Violet looked toward the Tower House, then she said, "Quick, look over there!"

The door was open just wide enough so that Miss Smith could look out. When she saw Violet, she called, "Who saved our house?"

"That boy, Benny. My brother," Violet said. "He ran to get the fire department to come."

"Which boy is Benny?" asked Miss Smith.

"Right here. Me," said Benny.

Miss Smith looked at him and said, "Good!" Then she went in and shut the door. The Aldens looked at each other.

Henry said, "Miss Smith isn't very friendly."

Jessie said, "I told you it would be slow. It will take more than a fire to make friends with Miss Smith. She has been shut up alone too long."

"Well, Ben, you didn't do it to be thanked," Henry said.

"No," answered Benny. He was very quiet. He was thinking.

As the Aldens drove back to the beach trailer, Jessie said, "I'm glad nobody set that fire. After that boy told us about breaking that window for nothing, I could believe almost anything."

"Right," agreed Henry. "I can't blame Miss Smith for not being very friendly."

Then Benny burst out, "You know what? I think there are two people living in Tower House! I don't think Miss Smith lives there all by herself."

"We know she has cats," Jessie said slowly.

"I don't mean the cats," Benny said firmly. "I think another person lives there, too."

"Everybody says she lives alone, Ben," argued Henry.

Violet asked, "What makes you think that, Benny?"

Benny answered quickly, "Don't you remember she said, 'Who saved *our* house?' Not *my* house. When she said that, she didn't mean the cats. I'm sure of it."

"Well, you may be right," said Jessie.

"Maybe I am," Benny agreed. "And maybe that locket belongs to this mysterious person, and that is why Miss Smith wouldn't take it."

"I begin to see!" Henry said, nodding. "If she took the locket, that would give her secret away!"

CHAPTER 7

Violet's Adventure

Benny woke very early next morning. He looked out and saw that the weather had changed. It was very windy. The waves were high and the sand was blowing.

Benny pulled on an old pair of pants and a sweatshirt. He wanted to race along the beach, barefoot, and have the whole place to himself.

Without waking Henry or the girls, Benny opened the door and slipped outside.

The very first thing, he stubbed his toe on a stone.

"Ow!" he exclaimed. "That stone wasn't there last night. Now who in the world would put a stone right in my way?"

Then suddenly he saw a piece of white paper blowing away. He raced after the paper.

The wind blew it high, then low. At last it dropped on the sand.

"Got you!" said Benny. He put his foot on it, until he could pick it up. "That stone I stepped on was holding you down."

Benny soon saw that the paper was a sheet of writing paper, folded in half. On the outside something was written in old-fashioned writing. Benny could hardly read it in the dim light, but at last he made out the words, "Thank you." Then he opened the paper and looked inside. He read the message twice. It did not seem to make any sense. It said, "All thanks you. We all thank you."

That was it. Benny turned the paper over. He folded it again. "Who wrote this?" he thought. "And it must be for us, right in front of our trailer. That sentence, 'All thanks you,' isn't even good English."

He started back to the trailer house. Now he looked around to see if anyone was in sight. The beach was empty from one end to the other.

"Perhaps there are footprints," Benny thought.

But all he found were his own barefoot tracks he had just made chasing the paper.

Near the door Benny found what he was looking for. There were three small footprints on the hard sand. "They look like a child's shoes," he thought.

Two footprints pointed toward the trailer, and one was made as the person turned to go toward the water. But that was all. Everything else was washed away by the tide. There was nothing to show where the nighttime visitor had come from or gone.

But Benny still had the note. He read it again. Then he opened the door of the trailer and found Henry and the girls just waking up.

"Look!" Benny called. "A new mystery!"

Everyone took turns looking at the note, reading it, and then looking out at the beach.

At last Jessie said, "Well, I don't know what to make of this."

"We can show it to Mr. Lee," Benny said.

"If he's out on a windy morning like this," Henry said. "The weather has changed."

"Let's have breakfast inside," Jessie suggested. "Ben, you sit where you can watch for Mr. Lee."

But although everyone watched, Mr. Lee and Richard did not come down the beach. There was not a sign of them. Jessie let the hot water for the tea grow cold. Everyone felt a bit sad and uneasy.

Benny still thought about the note. " 'All thanks you,' " he said. "That bothers me."

Henry said, "Let me see that note again. The writing is hard to read. Do you think it really says 'all'?"

"I don't know what else it could say," Benny answered. "I would really like to know what it means."

"We all would," Jessie said. "But I give up. I don't think we'll ever know what the message means or who was supposed to read it."

Benny folded the paper and put it in his pocket. "Let's go to town," he said. "It's too stormy to go swimming. There isn't much to do here."

Nobody else really wanted to say this, but they were restless not doing anything.

"Something may come up," Benny said. "But it is more likely to come up in Beachwood than out here."

"We'll just wait until after lunch, Benny," said

Jessie. "Then we'll go up to Beachwood."

After the lunch dishes were done, they all changed their clothes and climbed into Henry's car.

They were soon on Main Street in Beachwood, but Henry had a hard time parking the car.

"I forgot this was shopping day," said Henry, looking everywhere for a parking place. "I guess the windy weather made everybody decide to come to town."

At last, far down the Main Street, almost at the very end, Henry found room to park. In fact, there was space for two or three cars along the curb.

"One place is all I need," Henry said, laughing. He put a coin in the meter.

"Look at the crowd," Benny exclaimed. "Let's just walk down the street with the crowd. I didn't know Beachwood had so many people."

"It doesn't, Ben," Jessie told him. "You'll notice half this crowd comes in from the beaches. The town people are all pale, and the visitors are tanned."

"And the town people take their time and drive along slowly," Benny said. "But look at some of the beach people!"

"That's right," Henry agreed. "Those drivers expect you to keep out of their way. If you don't, too bad!"

The Aldens had worked their way down Main Street as far as the drugstore. The street was thick with cars, and people were looking for parking places and honking their horns. What a racket!

Henry and Benny, with Jessie between them, walked along quickly. But Violet stopped to look in a window.

Suddenly Violet cried out, "Oh, look! Look at that cat!"

And before Henry or anyone else could stop her, she ran out into the street. She threw her left hand high in the air to stop the cars coming toward her. There was a noise of grinding gears, and all the cars stopped with a jerk.

Paying no attention, Violet bent over and picked up an enormous gray cat. He was crouching in the dust of the street, and trembling all over.

With the cat safe in her arms, Violet ran back to the sidewalk.

"Did you see that?" a man asked his wife. "That girl risked her life for a cat. She could have been killed!"

Jessie and Henry took Violet between them and led her through the crowd. Violet had the big cat safe in her arms, and indeed the cat did not try to get away.

The drugstore clerk had come to the door of his store. He watched as the postman spoke to Violet.

The postman said, "That's Miss Smith's cat. She lives in Tower House. But I don't think she'll let you in."

"She'll let you in this time—when she sees you

coming with her cat," said the clerk.

People turned to look and smile at Violet. She was a pretty picture in her lavender shorts, a lavender scarf over her hair. And against the lavender was the great gray cat, with long soft fur and beautiful big eyes.

The cat lay still in Violet's arms, although she could feel its heart beating fast. He seemed to know that he was safe from all the noise.

The Aldens walked across to the Tower House, and this time Benny rapped. He did not have to rap again, for the door opened at once. There stood a new Mary Smith. She was very much upset and frightened.

"Oh, come in! Bring the cat in. I let him out! I am to blame," Miss Smith said all in one breath. "To think he could have been run over in the street!"

The cat seemed to be comfortable in Violet's arms. It did not move or try to get down.

When Miss Smith told Violet and Benny to go into the house, they did so. They looked quickly around the room. They both noticed a long black velvet curtain which hung from the ceiling to the floor at the end of the room. But they were amazed at Miss Smith. She was shaking, really shaking.

Violet said, "You'd feel better if you made a cup of hot tea. Why don't you get one? We'll be careful when we go out and not let your cat out again."

Miss Smith actually smiled at Violet. "Oh, I believe I will," she said. "That cat is Ali Baba the Third, and to think I nearly lost him! You stay just a minute. I don't want any tea."

Miss Smith went through the black curtain at the end of the room. She was careful not to let any light shine into the room beyond.

Violet looked about and noticed that the furniture was old and fine and the carpet was an oriental one. She still held the big cat.

Jessie and Henry had been a few steps behind Benny and Violet. When Miss Smith had asked them to come in, she had been too excited to notice Henry and Jessie. They were left out, on the other side of the door.

"We sure were left out in the cold," Henry said. "I wish we knew what was going on inside the Tower House."

"I thought Violet and Benny would be right out," Jessie said. "But I am sure they are all right."

"We'll wait, then try knocking," Henry decided.

Inside the house, Miss Smith soon came back to her guests. She was still upset. "I let him out!" she repeated. "I just opened the door a crack and out he went, flying. I let him out."

Benny and Violet could not understand this. But they were not going to leave Miss Smith until she felt better. Nobody could be less like a witch than Miss Smith!

"I love cats," said Violet. "And so does Benny."

"I see you do. I never saw that cat go to anybody, not even me. You must have a way with you. Do you have a cat?"

"No, we have a dog," replied Violet, smiling.

Benny said, "I can just see Watch if we brought home a cat. He's a dog that doesn't like cats."

"Most dogs don't," said Miss Smith, still trembling.

If Violet and Benny had known it, Miss Smith had talked more in the last five minutes than she did in most weeks. She couldn't seem to stop saying, "I am to blame. I'm the one who let him out."

Violet still held the cat. She said, "Don't blame yourself so much. Look, here is the cat, safe in the house. And he's beginning to purr. Nobody else, surely, is blaming you."

But Miss Smith certainly acted as if someone else was blaming her. She stared at the cat and said, "I never saw Ali Baba friendly with anyone before. He's a very wild cat."

Benny said, "He knows Violet loves him. Animals know when anyone really likes them."

It was odd that neither Benny nor Violet thought once of the locket and the picture of the cat in it. But they were too busy thinking of Miss Smith and her troubles. Then, out of the corner of his eye, Benny saw the black curtain move.

"That is no cat," Benny thought. "I'm sure there are two people here, just as I thought."

Violet had the same idea. Miss Smith disappeared behind the curtain again for a minute. When she came back, she said, "Would you do something for me, little girl?"

Violet did not feel that she was a little girl, but she said, "Of course. I hope it is something I can do."

"What can Miss Smith want?" Benny wondered.

"Come back tomorrow morning when the sun is just right. About ten o'clock. Can you do that? Will you? And wear the same clothes."

Violet was too surprised to speak, so Benny said, "Yes, she can."

Miss Smith seemed better now, and Violet put the cat down. "I'll see you tomorrow at ten," she said. "Good-bye."

The minute Violet and Benny joined Jessie and Henry they began to tell them all that had happened.

"Miss Smith said I was to come when the light was right," Violet said. "I can't guess what she means."

Benny had a fine idea. "I think Miss Smith wants to paint a picture of Violet with the cat in her arms."

They all agreed. Jessie said, "Violet was certainly a picture with all that gray and violet color."

"What a story we'll have for Mr. Lee," Benny said. "I'm sure he thought we'd never get inside the Tower House."

In all the excitement, Benny and Violet forgot about the cat's name. After all, a great deal had happened in a short time.

The next morning Mr. Lee was surprised at all the news. He thought exactly as the Aldens did. When they told him of Miss Smith's request, he agreed that probably Violet was going to sit for her picture with the cat in her arms. "Otherwise," remarked Mr. Lee, "she wouldn't have told Violet what color to wear."

At exactly ten o'clock Henry stopped the blue car in front of the Tower House and Violet got out. Miss Smith opened the door before she had time to knock.

"Go in, please," Miss Smith said. She pushed back the black curtain.

Violet found herself in an artist's studio. Sunshine came in through the large back window, and there was light everywhere. And sure enough, there was another person! She came out of the shadows.

She was a tiny little woman, dressed in a smock, all covered with paint. She looked sharply at Violet.

"Sit here," she said suddenly. "Good of you to come. Take up Ali Baba."

Now Violet never picked up a cat. She always waited for the cat to come to her. She explained this now as she saw the cat lying asleep on a silk cushion.

She did not wait long. Ali stretched himself and jumped lightly into her lap.

"A marvel," said the artist. She wasted no time but began to draw very quickly on the paper on the easel.

"You don't have to sit still," she said gruffly. "Don't look at Ali. Look at me."

Violet obeyed. The cat settled down in her arms exactly as he had done the day before. He felt safe.

"How will you get home, child?" asked the little woman.

"Oh, my brother Henry is waiting with the car. They are all waiting."

"Who is 'all'?"

"Well, my sister Jessie, Henry, my big brother, and Benny, my younger brother. There are four of us."

"Four of you?" said the little woman. "Yes, that's right. A loving family, eh?"

"Oh, yes."

"I never saw one myself," said the artist.

"You should meet mine," Violet exclaimed. How sad it must be, Violet thought, to live all one's life and never know a loving family.

Ali had gone to sleep. His head was lying sideways, and he had stopped purring.

Suddenly Violet asked, "Do you have other cats?"

"Oh, yes. I have ten cats. I like cats better than people, you see. I try not to have anything to do with people."

Violet thought about that. Here was someone who did not want to make friends. If Ali had not escaped from the house, Violet would never have been invited to come in.

Without even having begun to paint, the artist said, "That's all. Come tomorrow, child." And she handed Violet a note that said, "Please be ready for me at 10. Thank you."

"I will be," Violet said. She started to put Ali Baba back on the cushion, talking to him all the time. He growled softly. He was very comfortable and did not want to be moved.

"I'll be back tomorrow to hold you," Violet promised. She did not even try to look at the picture. She knew it was not done and she would have to wait.

The artist called, "Mary, please let this little girl out. We are finished for today." And to Violet she said with great charm, "Thank you, my dear, for coming."

"Just a minute, Ruth," Violet heard Miss Smith answer. And in a moment she appeared and led Violet to the door.

"You've made Miss Lane and me happy," Miss Smith said quickly. Her cheeks were pink as she spoke, and suddenly Violet knew that this was a very shy person. How wrong everyone in Beachwood was about Miss Mary Smith!

CHAPTER 8

An Invitation

Violet was hardly in the car when the questions began.

"What happened in there?" Benny asked.

"You're all right?" Jessie wanted to know.

"Miss Smith didn't scare you today, did she?" asked Henry.

Violet laughed. "It was all a surprise," she said. "It's hard to know where to begin."

"Begin at the beginning," said Benny.

"First," Violet said, "we were wrong about Miss Smith. So is everyone else, too. She isn't an artist at all."

"But—" Benny said.

"Miss Lane, Miss Ruth Lane, is the artist," Violet explained. "She's a tiny little woman. That big window at the back of the Tower House is the room where she works."

Henry said, "Wait a minute. You said Ruth Lane. We know the house was owned by the Lane family. But no one ever said anything about a Ruth Lane."

Benny said, "Ruth Lane—R.L. There we are! Those are the initials on the locket. Now we're getting somewhere."

Jessie said, "So there are two women who live in the Tower House."

"And ten cats," Violet added. "It's funny, you don't notice the way the house smells after you've been inside for a little bit."

The talking stopped for a moment. Then Benny said, "So it looks as if Miss Smith keeps house for Miss Lane."

"Yes," Violet agreed. "Miss Lane says she doesn't like people. She just likes cats. But she was very nice to me. Maybe she surprised herself and liked having company."

"She probably thinks you are all right because you saved her cat," Benny said.

"Did Miss Lane paint your picture?" asked Henry.

Violet shook her head. "No, she just made a pencil drawing while I held Ali. She wants me to come back tomorrow at the same time. She gave me this little note. I guess she doesn't want me to forget."

"Let's see," Benny said. He unfolded the paper Violet gave him and read, " 'Please be ready for me at 10. Thank you.' "

Suddenly Benny began to feel in all of his pockets until at last he pulled out another paper. He unfolded it and put it beside Miss Lane's note.

"Look at that!" he said. "I think I understand something now."

All the Aldens looked at the two notes.

"The same kind of paper!" Violet said.

"And the same writing, I'm almost sure," Henry said, beginning to smile. "See the 'thank you'?"

Benny said, "That's what I think. But what about that funny sentence, 'All thanks you'? Miss Lane wouldn't write that, would she, Violet?"

Then Violet made a clever guess. "Let me see

those notes," she said. "Look, Benny, the word isn't *all*. It's the name *Ali*. The letter *i* looks like the letter *l*."

Benny said, "Then the note says '*Ali* thanks you. We all thank you.' And Ali Baba is Miss Lane's favorite cat, so she must have written the note and put it by our trailer. Well, that's another mystery solved."

"Not quite," Henry said. "That thank-you note was written after the grass fire in the Tower House yard. But Miss Lane and Miss Smith didn't know who we were or where we were living. How did the note get delivered?"

Violet said, "I don't know. But the note fits with the ladies being so shy. I really never met anyone as shy as Miss Lane and Miss Smith."

"I wish Miss Lane wanted to paint my picture," Benny said. "Maybe I could find out how she knew us and where we lived at the beach."

Just before sunset that evening, Mr. Lee walked down the beach with Richard. He did not have his metal-finder with him. He was interested in hearing about Violet's visit.

When he had heard all the news, he said, "There are famous paintings of cats, and the artist's name is Ruth Lane. There are a lot of people who buy and collect those paintings. In fact I've seen cat portraits by Ruth Lane in New York shops. But I just happen to like dogs better than cats."

Mr. Lee patted Richard, and the big dog wagged his tail.

The Aldens walked with Mr. Lee along the beach until he was nearly home.

"I don't think I'll be taking any midnight walks," Mr. Lee said as they told him goodnight. "I mean I feel I'll sleep well tonight," he added quickly.

As the Aldens walked back toward the trailer, Benny said, "I wonder what Mr. Lee meant about not taking a midnight walk. That remark just slipped out. He seemed sorry right after he said it."

Henry laughed at Benny and said, "There you go again. Still looking for mysteries."

But Benny was stubborn. "Well, there are still a few mysteries. One big one is why Miss Smith doesn't want that locket. It just has to have something to do with her or Miss Lane."

Jessie said, 'Tomorrow's another day. Maybe we'll find the answer then. I think it's time for bed."

On her second visit to Miss Lane, Violet knew what to expect. She knew that the little artist had a sharp tongue, and she didn't mind too much. Violet felt sorry for the little lady who had shut herself off from people.

As Violet sat down in the chair, Miss Lane said, "Never mind holding the cat. I can paint him in any time. I've drawn your arms."

Then Violet noticed that Miss Lane was painting today, not drawing. She worked quickly, almost as if she were painting a house, Violet thought.

"You paint fast," Violet remarked.

"I have to," answered the artist. "This paint dries in twenty minutes. It's not oil. It's acrylic paint. Look right at me. Never mind smiling."

This amused Violet. She couldn't help smiling a little. She knew Miss Lane was painting her eyes.

Suddenly without any warning, Miss Lane said, "Good. That's enough. Come day after tomorrow."

Violet got up and started to go out. Miss Lane said, "Look at the picture if you want to."

"Oh, may I?" asked Violet, surprised. She took one look at the picture. "That looks exactly like me!" she said.

"Yes, it does. Today was easy. Everything came right, and the colors are just right." Miss Lane looked very much pleased.

Violet said, "It must be wonderful to paint so well. You must be very happy."

Miss Lane shrugged but said nothing.

Violet asked, "Will you sell this?"

"Probably."

"I hope people won't know it is my picture," Violet exclaimed. "You aren't going to put my name on it, are you?"

"No," Miss Lane said gruffly. "The name of the picture is 'Girl with Cat.' "

"Oh, thank you," Violet said.

"I'll do more than that," Miss Lane went on. "I'll change the mouth so the picture doesn't look like you. I've never changed a picture before for anybody."

"Oh, that's very kind of you!" Violet burst out. "I know an artist doesn't like to change his picture."

Miss Lane had certainly never been called kind before in her life. But this time she did feel kind—and it was odd, she liked it.

Violet said, "Please don't change the picture. My grandfather might want to buy it. I do wish you'd paint Benny. But nobody could paint him. He's never still a minute."

"I expect he can look straight at me for one minute and then later for another minute?"

"Oh, yes. He'd try. He might not like the idea of sitting still to have his picture painted, but he would do it for Grandfather."

"Who is this grandfather?" Miss Lane asked.

"Grandfather? Well, we live with him. Our parents died years ago. He is James Henry Alden, and my brother Henry is Henry James Alden. He is the best grandfather anyone ever had."

"You do sound like a very happy family," Miss Lane said, and Violet thought her voice had a sad sound. The sharpness that had been there earlier was gone.

Violet said slowly, "I have an idea I hope you will like. Here at the beach we have picnics all the time.

We like to eat outdoors. Couldn't you and Miss Smith take the noon hour and come to have lunch with us? It is really not very far. I'd love to have you know Henry and Jessie and Benny."

Miss Lane shook her head. "No, I don't think we'd better."

"Oh, dear!" Violet said. "We'd all like it so much. I'll tell you how to make it easier. Henry will come for you about noon, and you won't have to do a thing but get in the car."

Something in Violet's voice and in her smile must have touched Miss Lane. She said, "It is very kind of you. Yes, we can come after all. What time did you say?"

"Well, I said noon, but let's call it quarter of twelve. By that time Benny will be shouting for lunch. He is always hungry. I'll tell Jessie."

"Don't you have to ask her?"

"Oh, no. Jessie is the housekeeper. She expects things like this—company for lunch."

Miss Lane called Miss Smith and said, "Mary, we are going out for lunch today."

Miss Smith looked very surprised.

Violet saw her family waiting in the blue car. She said, "Oh, do please come and meet my family."

The two women went with Violet to the door. In an instant both Benny and Henry were out of the car. Violet introduced everyone, and the ladies said "How do you do" to each one and nodded stiffly.

The Aldens tried not to look too surprised to see the two women no one in Beachwood knew.

When the blue car was well on its way, Violet said, "Jessie, I've asked Miss Lane and Miss Smith to come for a picnic lunch—today."

"And are they really coming?" asked Benny.

"Yes, they are!" Violet answered.

Henry laughed and said, "Violet, sometimes you can really surprise us."

"It wasn't so hard," Violet said. "I think no one has ever tried to ask the ladies before. People have thought they were unfriendly. They're really just shy."

"And independent, too," Jessie said. "They have thought they could get along without people."

Benny said, "Have you ever noticed that cats are like that, too? They are always independent and like to be free. They don't make the kind of pets dogs do."

"Perhaps that's why the Tower House is a home for ten cats," Henry said. "But I'd still like to know if Miss Lane and Miss Smith left us that note."

CHAPTER 9

Answers at Last

Jessie said, "For this picnic party I'm going to make sandwiches. I don't want to take time to make a fire on the beach and cook hamburgers. I'll make ham sandwiches and tuna and—"

"And peanut butter," finished Benny.

"Right. And we'll have quarts of pink lemonade and cookies—everyone likes that."

Violet said slowly, "The ladies may like coffee, the way Grandfather does."

"Then I'll make some hot coffee."

"We are lucky," said Henry. "We have had pleasant weather almost every day. Today is just right for a picnic."

Just at quarter of twelve, Henry's blue car stopped in front of the Tower House. At the same moment the door of the house opened and Miss Lane came out. Miss Smith followed.

Violet and Benny had come with Henry. "We left Jessie at the beach," Benny said, jumping out of the car. "She's the housekeeper. Miss Lane, you climb in beside Henry, and Miss Smith will sit in the back with Violet and me."

Miss Lane said, "We could have walked and saved you all this trouble."

"Oh, but it's much more fun to ride," said Benny. "You don't get so much sand in your shoes, either."

"What if people see us going for a ride this way?" Miss Smith asked. "What will they think?"

Miss Lane said, "Don't be silly, Mary. Let them think what they like. We don't have to speak to anyone else."

Violet thought suddenly, "This is a big step for these ladies. And it certainly would be a surprise if the people in Beachwood knew. Maybe little boys would stop talking about witches living in the Tower House."

Down the short back road they went. Henry
stopped the car right behind the trailer house.

"Come in," called Jessie. "We want you to see the
house."

Violet put her hand lightly on Miss Lane's arm.
"This way," she said.

The two women had never seen a mobile home
from the inside. Miss Smith liked the tiny kitchen
with a place for everything. Miss Lane liked the
living room which changed into a bedroom at
night.

"You see, it's quite roomy," Jessie said.

So, very slowly, the Aldens got their company outdoors onto the sand. The water was very blue and
beautiful, and there were now two chairs and a table
and a beach umbrella. There was even a little breeze
off the water, and it was very comfortable.

Benny threw himself on the sand and said, "Let's
eat, Jessie."

"Right, Ben. I was just going to ask you to help
bring out the things. You get right up. Take a plate
of sandwiches in each hand, Benny, and then come
back."

Benny said, "Do I have to take one in each hand, Jessie? Suppose I carry one on my head."

"Oh, Benny, just don't drop them," Jessie answered.

Benny said, "You see, ladies, there is a toothpick and a little sign telling you what kind of sandwiches we have today. This one says Ham, and this says Tuna, and of course mine says Peanut Butter and Jelly."

Benny's nonsense was good for the two visitors. They had to laugh, and when they saw the sandwiches, they forgot to feel stiff and shy.

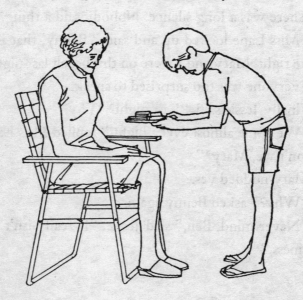

Miss Lane and Miss Smith sat at the table where they could see the blue water and the Aldens. They could not see the crowd of people behind them. They could hear, but the noise seemed far away.

Miss Smith said quietly, "This pink lemonade reminds me of picnics when I was a little girl."

Miss Lane had taken her fourth sandwich. She said, "I had forgotten how lovely a picnic can be. Sandwiches and sweet pickles and hardboiled eggs seem to go with a picnic."

Benny said, "I forgot how swell they are myself. And *you* haven't been on the beach for years."

There was a long silence. Nobody said a thing. At last Miss Lane looked up and said, "Benny, that isn't quite right. Mary and I were on this beach last night."

Everyone was too surprised to speak.

Finally Jessie said, "Last night? Why?"

"We come almost every night," replied Miss Lane. "Don't we, Mary?"

Mary nodded yes.

"Why?" asked Benny again.

"Never mind, Ben," said Jessie. "It really isn't our business."

"I know it isn't," Benny said. "But I'm making it my business. I really want to know. I know it isn't polite to ask."

Miss Smith suddenly said, "I don't blame you a bit. I think you are a very polite boy."

Miss Lane nodded this time. "I don't blame you, either. We don't want to see people or talk to people so we walk on the beach at night. We like the middle of the night. That way we get some exercise and fresh air, and we can sleep in the daytime if we want to."

"You might call us night people, just like our cats," Miss Smith said.

Miss Lane said, "It was on one of those nights that I lost my locket."

"Oh, your locket with R.L. on the cover!" Benny exclaimed. "Wait and I will get it for you. I put it in a safe hiding place inside." In a moment Benny dropped the gold locket into Miss Lane's hand. "We know now the R.L. is for Ruth Lane."

"No," said Miss Lane, shaking her head. "It really doesn't stand for Ruth Lane. It just *happened* that way. It first belonged to my grandmother and her name was Rachel Lester. Then my mother had the locket and her name happened to be Rose Lawrence. Then I got it, and my name happened to be Ruth Lane."

"Isn't that a surprising story!" Benny said.

"Yes, three generations and all R.L., but for three different names. I always thought it was very strange. And I am so glad to have the locket back. It belongs on this gold chain I am wearing."

Sure enough, Miss Lane had a thick braided gold chain hanging almost to her waist. She took it off and slipped the chain through the locket.

"Found in the sand," said Benny. "When do you think you lost it?"

"Oh, just before you came to the trailer. We looked for it the night your aunt and uncle went away and before you came. But every night we walk the beach."

"Our midnight walkers!" Benny exclaimed. "You walk very fast."

"Indeed yes."

"Does anyone ever follow you?" asked Benny.

"Oh, yes, many times somebody follows us. We probably look like men because we wear old jackets and pants. Only just the other night a man in a cape followed us. But we knew who he was, so we didn't mind."

"You knew who he was?" repeated Benny.

"Oh, yes, he is a famous writer, and he lives down the beach in the last cottage. He always wears a cape."

"Do you know his name?" asked Violet.

"Oh, yes. Everybody even in Beachwood knows him. He is Daniel Lee."

The Aldens looked at each other. "We know him, too," said Henry. "It was his metal-finder that found your locket."

"No," said Miss Lane, really smiling now. "It was Benny who found my locket."

"So it was," agreed Jessie. "I guess everyone knew who Mr. Lee was except us. And we really thought we knew him best of all."

"How did you get to know him?" asked Miss Lane.

"He came by and we spoke to him," replied Benny. "We just said 'Good morning,' and he said said 'Good morning.' It's easy to make friends."

Miss Lane said thoughtfully, "It's easy for you, Benny. You are like that. I wouldn't know how to begin after all these years."

"You have already begun," said Violet gently.

Henry said, "We did see both of you walking along the beach at night. Of course we thought you were two men. We saw the man in a cape following you."

Miss Smith said rather shyly, "I think Mr. Lee likes to feel he is looking after us. Old people don't sleep very well at night, and they like to be useful."

Benny said, "I believe you are right. But I have a question to ask. I found footprints in the sand one morning and this note that said 'Ali thanks you. We all thank you.' Did you put it there, or was it a child?"

Miss Lane and Miss Smith looked at each other and really laughed.

Miss Lane said, "We might as well tell you the whole story. Mary and I aren't used to talking much. We don't even talk much to each other. But we both began to think we hadn't properly thanked you for saving our house from the fire. All Mary said was

'Good.' And that wasn't really enough. So I went down early and put the note under a stone. It wasn't a child who put the note there. See! I have small feet." She showed them her tiny feet. After all, she was a tiny person.

"Well, that's settled," said Benny. "Now one more question. How did you know where we lived?"

Miss Smith answered, "I knew there were four of you. I looked out of the big back window the day of the fire and saw the blue car. We had seen this car parked behind your trailer. So we put two and two together."

Benny said, "And I thought I was the only one who put two and two together!"

Everyone laughed.

"I understand a lot of things now," Benny said. "But, Miss Smith, why wouldn't you take the locket back when we brought it to your house the first time?"

Miss Smith did not answer right away. Then she said slowly, "Well, you took me by surprise. I didn't have much time to think. And it wasn't my locket. If I took it, you would know it belonged to somebody else, with R.L. on the cover. And then you might have found out that I did not live alone."

"I think I see," said Jessie. "People didn't understand you, and you didn't understand them."

"Maybe," said Miss Lane. "But we really must go home now. Violet, will you come again tomorrow so that I can finish your picture?"

"I will," Violet said happily.

"I'll take you home," Henry said.

"Oh, no," said Miss Lane. "We can walk."

Henry laughed. He said, "I wouldn't think of letting you ladies walk that far."

"When we walk at least two miles every night?"

"Even so, this time you are going to ride," said Henry.

CHAPTER 10

New Trick for an Old Dog

When the last day at the beach came, Henry said, "Let's telephone and ask Grandfather to come down for our last beach picnic."

"He can meet our new friends—Mr. Lee, Miss Lane, and Miss Smith," said Benny.

"And Miss Lane has finished the picture," said Violet.

Jessie said, "We'll have a picnic for everyone. I'm sure the ladies will enjoy it."

Mr. Alden said he would be delighted to drive the station wagon down to the picnic. Benny and Violet could drive back with him, and Henry and Jessie could come in the blue car.

Jessie took charge of getting ready. She said, "You boys really sweep out the living room for Aunt Jane and Uncle Andy. We want to leave their trailer as clean as we found it. Violet can dust, and I'll make sandwiches."

Everyone bustled around. It did not take long to get everything in perfect order.

Jessie said, "We'll put four chairs under the beach umbrella. We'll use the table, too. Grandfather hates to hold a cup and saucer and a knife and fork and eat at the same time."

"So do I," Benny said.

"Well then, you sit up at the table, too," replied Jessie. "We want everyone to be comfortable."

Just then the station wagon pulled up behind the trailer. "Anybody home?" called a familiar voice.

"Grandfather!" cried Violet, "Come in."

At almost the same moment, a voice from the beach called, "Are you expecting visitors?"

"Oh, Mr. Lee, come in," Jessie said. "Grandfather just came, too."

"Hi, Dan!" Mr. Alden said.

"Hi, James," answered Mr. Lee, smiling.

"Do you two know each other?" asked Benny, very much surprised.

"Well, I should say we do," replied Mr. Alden. "Dan and I have been friends in New York for many years. He knows all about you, and he enjoyed becoming acquainted."

"Did you ask him to keep an eye on us?" demanded Benny.

"I did not. I always trust you to manage your own affairs and to come to the right person if you have any trouble."

"It's all my fault," said Mr. Lee. "I couldn't keep away. Every day I looked forward to coming down to visit. It was a pleasure and I am delighted it all turned out so well."

"Couldn't have been better," said Grandfather.

"Yes, I can think of a way it might be even better," said Mr. Lee, taking his usual chair. Looking at Mr. Alden he laughed and said, "This is my chair, James."

"Yes, and this is mine. No sitting down on the sand for me. I might get down, but I don't know how I would get up again."

"I know," said Benny. "Henry and I would pull you up, that's what."

"I have no doubt of that," said Mr. Alden, and he looked off at the blue water. "And now what was your idea, Dan?"

Mr. Lee answered at once, "Ruth Lane is a good artist. Her paintings are sold all over New York. A great many people come here in the summer, and many of them must like Ruth Lane's pictures of cats. I think Ruth Lane should have an art exhibit here in Beachwood."

"That's an interesting idea," said Mr. Alden. "How did you know Miss Lane was here when no one else did?"

"Well, I have been coming here for a long time," answered Mr. Lee. "I heard Miss Lane was living and working somewhere near here. I guessed she was in the old family home, the Tower House. But I knew she never welcomed people. People never saw her, just her friend and housekeeper, Miss Smith."

"How did you find Miss Lane really did live in the Tower House?" Benny asked.

"Well, I thought the ladies had to go outdoors

sometimes just for a change from the house. I found they liked long walks on the beach at night. I thought if I followed them, Miss Lane might possibly talk to me. But she wouldn't."

Violet said, "Miss Lane knew who you were. And I think she was rather pleased you were following her."

Grandfather said, "To go back to the matter of the art exhibit. Do you think Miss Lane would like that? The children seem to think she is shy."

"She is shy. But I think your grandchildren have helped her see that people are friendly if you only give them a chance."

Benny said, "Miss Lane and Miss Smith know a lot of things that aren't true have been said about them in Beachwood. Kids say an old witch with a hundred cats lives in the Tower House. One boy even broke a window just for the fun of it."

"That's true," Mr. Lee said.

"Miss Lane may be shy," Violet added, "but she knows she is a good painter."

"She sells her pictures, all right," said Mr. Lee. "I should think she would agree to an exhibit. But there is another reason why I think she would be delighted."

"And what is that?" asked Mr. Alden.

"Suppose I told her that the money the exhibit earns would be used for a shelter for stray cats? That is the kind of thing she would like very much."

"That is the best idea!" said Jessie. "I'm sure she will think it is a fine idea, too. But I didn't know she had enough pictures for an exhibit."

"She has," said Mr. Lee. "There are dozens in New York. Then, James, I think if you asked, some people would loan pictures they have already bought. This could be a very interesting exhibit."

Violet said, "I think Miss Lane would want to show the picture she painted of Ali and me."

"And that would help everyone in Beachwood understand Miss Lane better," Benny said.

"I think so, too," agreed Jessie.

"Well, I guess Henry can go for the ladies now," said Mr. Lee.

"He's already gone," Jessie told him.

When the blue car arrived, Miss Lane was carrying a basket. She said, "I brought a present for

Violet." Then suddenly she saw Mr. Lee. She said in a low voice, "Hello, Dan. We haven't met for many years."

"But now we are neighbors," said Mr. Lee, "and I hope we'll meet often. What is in the basket? It seems to be something alive."

"It is," replied Miss Lane. "You see, Violet was willing to let me paint her picture."

Violet looked at the basket—it moved a trifle.

Miss Lane opened the basket and drew out a kitten —a perfectly white kitten with long, soft fur, blue eyes, and a look like a puffball.

"Oh, you lovely little thing!" cried Violet, her eyes shining. "May I hold him?"

Miss Lane set the kitten down on the sand. He sat there with his small tail out straight behind him. Violet took the tiny tail and curled it around him. The little cat instantly uncurled it and curled it up again, just exactly the way Violet had placed it.

"Look at that," Benny said. "He wants to do it himself."

Violet replied, "That's like all cats. I ought to have remembered. I am so used to dogs now."

Then the little puffball began to climb up the front of Violet's blouse. His tiny claws were like needles.

Violet pulled him off, but he went right up again. He seemed to know he was Violet's cat, just as old Watch knew he was Jessie's dog.

"What's his name?" asked Benny. "Or hasn't he a name yet?"

Miss Lane answered, "Yes, his name is Sugar Cookie. He's a registered cat. His mother is Bluebell the Third and his grandmother was White Clover the Second."

Violet pulled a blue string across the sand. The kitten followed it like a little wild tiger, biting it and tossing it in the air. Every motion was beautiful.

Miss Lane watched the kitten so closely that everyone began to watch Miss Lane. She saw the kitten's motions just as she would paint them.

"There is a second present, and it is for Mr. Alden," said Miss Lane. She took the paper off Violet's portrait. It was a lovely thing, and it looked exactly like Violet.

Mr. Alden was delighted. He kept looking from the picture to the slender girl and back again. He was wondering if Miss Lane would like the idea of an exhibit.

"Sugar Cookie, let's eat," said Benny. "How would you like some warm milk?"

Jessie went in to warm some milk, and Miss Lane sniffed the air. "That coffee smells good," she said.

Benny and Henry brought out plates of sandwiches and the pickles and cups for the hot coffee. For a few minutes it was busy and then it was very quiet as everyone began to eat.

After his second sandwich, Grandfather looked at Mr. Lee and raised his eyebrows in a question. Mr. Lee nodded.

Mr. Alden began very slowly. "Miss Lane, we have an idea for you and for everyone interested in pictures—and in stray cats, too."

At this last word, Miss Lane looked up at Mr. Alden. She was most interested in the word cats, stray cats.

Then Mr. Alden explained about the idea of a shelter for cats, a place where stray cats could be kept until good homes were found for them.

"I'd be very much interested in that," said Miss Lane. "But there must be a catch somewhere."

"There is!" exclaimed Benny. "You're smart, Miss Lane."

"It isn't really a catch," explained Mr. Lee. "Of course we must raise money to run such a shelter. You could give a one-man show with nothing but your own paintings. There'd be a small admission charge. The money would go to the shelter. Perhaps people who like cats would come."

"Perhaps people who like paintings but don't care for cats would come," Jessie added.

"You are all very clever," said Miss Lane, nodding. "You all know my weak spot. I may agree to this plan."

"Oh, I wish you would!" said Violet.

Sugar Cookie was tired out. He had gone to sleep in Violet's lap, one paw still around the blue string.

"If *you* wish me to, I will," said Miss Lane. "Your portrait is the best one I have ever done. Do you mind having it shown?"

Violet said, "No, I don't mind. I should think I might, but I don't."

Benny said, "I wouldn't mind, but I'm surprised at Violet. Usually she minds things like that."

The sandwiches were fast disappearing. The hardboiled eggs were all gone. The pickles were gone.

After the cookies were gone, Mr. Lee said good-bye. Grandfather watched him as he walked down the beach. He did not have Richard with him or his metal-finder.

Grandfather said, "Dan is exactly like me."

"Oh, no, Grandfather," said Violet, "not just exactly!"

"He thinks the way I do," said Grandfather. "He wants to get things done, quick, right off. He doesn't waste any time. You mark my words, he already has the whole art show planned. He knows exactly the people he will invite to help. And I am sure he has a place picked out for the animal shelter, too, and maybe a manager in mind. He probably wants you, Miss Lane, to paint a special picture to help advertise the center."

"I will, you know," Miss Lane said. "And now Mary and I must go. I know you all want to start for home. And I have to tell Bluebell why I took her kitten away. She has another, anyway, so she won't mind too much."

The Aldens left Grandfather sitting in his chair while they took the two ladies home. They wanted to say good-bye for now and to talk about other visits in the future.

Miss Lane had tears in her eyes when she said good-bye to Violet. "You've helped me more than you know," she said in a low voice.

"Don't forget Ali had to run away so that Violet could get to know you," Benny said.

They had to smile at that. Then the women disappeared into the tower.

Nobody spoke all the way back to the trailer until they saw Mr. Alden drawing a picture in the sand with his cane.

"I bet you have some ideas about the animal shelter," called Benny.

"Right," agreed Grandfather. "You come and get these chairs, Ben, and we'll go home."

The bags were soon ready. Jessie put the food that was left in a large basket to take home. They looked around the trailer home. It was all ready for Aunt Jane and Uncle Andy to enjoy again.

Grandfather, Benny, and Violet with her kitten went in the first car. Henry and Jessie followed in the blue car.

As they came near home, Violet said, "Now the most important thing is Watch. We simply cannot hurt his feelings. I'm sure he won't like Sugar Cookie. We'll have to think of some way to get him to like a kitten."

Benny said, "Make him think the kitten is his idea. He will like it if he thinks Sugar Cookie is his kitten."

Violet laughed. "How can we do that, Ben? You tell me."

But Benny could not think of a way.

Sugar Cookie found a way himself. He didn't know any better. He expected everyone to be his friend.

Watch was stretched out in the front hall. When he heard the cars stop, he stood up on his four feet and barked a welcome. He did not move. He was getting old.

The family came into the hall. Violet set the white kitten on the floor. In a second, Sugar Cookie ran to Watch, crying meow, me-ow in his baby voice. He had never seen a dog.

Watch had seen cats before, but never one like this. Sugar Cookie walked around Watch's front paws, rubbing his head against the old dog. The kitten certainly liked him.

Watch lay down. The kitten, tired out, turned around three times and lay down between the dog's front feet. Watch looked up at Violet as if to say, "Now I've got a friend of my own."

Violet exclaimed, "Oh, Watch, you've changed, and I'm so glad."

Mr. Alden laughed. He said, "This is a good end to a very pleasant adventure at the beach."

"Not the end, Grandfather," said Benny. "This is just the beginning of the end."

About the Author

GERTRUDE CHANDLER WARNER discovered when she was teaching that many readers who like an exciting story could find no books that were both easy and fun to read. She decided to try to meet this need, and her first book, *The Boxcar Children*, quickly proved she had succeeded.

Miss Warner drew on her own experiences to write the mystery. As a child she spent hours watching trains go by on the tracks opposite her family home. She often dreamed about what it would be like to set up housekeeping in a caboose or freight car—the situation the Alden children find themselves in.

When Miss Warner received requests for more adventures involving Henry, Jessie, Violet, and Benny Alden, she began additional stories. In each, she chose a special setting and introduced unusual or eccentric characters who liked the unpredictable.

While the mystery element is central to each of Miss Warner's books, she never thought of them as strictly juvenile mysteries. She liked to stress the Aldens' independence and resourcefulness and their solid New England devotion to using up and making do. The Aldens go about most of their adventures with as little adult supervision as possible—something else that delights young readers.

Miss Warner lived in Putnam, Connecticut, until her death in 1979. During her lifetime, she received hundreds of letters from girls and boys telling her how much they liked her book. And so she continued the Aldens' adventures, writing a total of nineteen books in the Boxcar Children series.